Connell

Dedications

"If we hope for what we do not yet have, we wait for it patiently."
For my parents, my siblings, and the children who inspired this story—
Samantha, Sebastian, Jeremy and Alexander—*David Seow*
To Asmara and Kazymir, thank you for your help and inspiration—*Olga Marie Polunin*

Cultural Background

This mythical tale draws upon Chinese and Asian cultural traditions and practices. Life at an imperial court was extremely rigid and formal. Also regular activities would have included lavish banquets, opera, and poetry. Therefore it would not be surprising for a little boy to wish to experience a world that is less stuffy and yearn for a simpler more fun way of life, even if only for a short time.

The Chinese are famous for their exotic culinary delights including bird's nest soup and jellyfish noodles. Bird's nest soup, a classic Chinese specialty, is a nutritious and healing delicacy, made from the nest of an Asian bird similar to the swift. Jellyfish noodles consist of shredded jellyfish, which is tasteless but very crunchy, and is eaten with a delicious sauce. The Littlest Emperor takes part in a dragon dance which is an important festive tradition in China, especially at Chinese New Year and other major festivals. The dragon can be very long and made of wood, cloth and paper, with poles attached to the dragon's belly. During the performance, performers hold the poles and raise the dragon, and this grand dance starts with the beats of roaring drums.

Published by Tuttle Publishing,
an imprint of Periplus Editions (HK) Ltd
with editorial offices at 153 Milk Street,
Boston, Massachusetts 02109 and 130 Joo
Seng Road #06-01/03, Singapore 368357

Text © David Seow, 2004
Illustrations © Olga Marie Polunin, 2004
All rights reserved

LCC Card No: 2003110861
ISBN 0-8048-3529-2
First printing, 2004

Printed in Singapore

08 07 06 05 04
6   5   4   3   2   1

Distributed by:

Japan
Tuttle Publishing
Yaekari Building, 3F
5-4-12 Osaki, Shinagawa-ku,
Tokyo 141-0032
Tel: (03) 5437 0171, Fax: (03) 5437 0755
Email: tuttle-sales@gol.com

North America, Latin America & Europe
Tuttle Publishing
364 Innovation Drive
North Clarendon, VT 05759-9436
Tel: (802) 773 8930, Fax: (802) 773 6993
Email: info@tuttlepublishing.com
Website: www.tuttlepublishing.com

Asia Pacific
Berkeley Books Pte Ltd
130 Joo Seng Road #06-01
Singapore 368357
Tel: (65) 6280 1330, Fax: (65) 6280 6290
Email: inquiries@periplus.com.sg

The Littlest Emperor

By David Seow

Illustrations by Olga Marie Polunin

TUTTLE PUBLISHING
Boston • Rutland, Vermont • Tokyo

A long time ago, in the largest and most beautiful kingdom in the world, the Littlest Emperor ruled.

3

Although he was the littlest of emperors, he had the biggest, kindest and wisest heart, and always made sure everyone had a warm house, nice clothes, and plenty of good things to eat.

One day everyone in his kingdom had everything they ever needed and the Littlest Emperor grew rather sad because he realized there was nothing left for him to do. Scratching his head he sighed, "My work is done. What shall I do now?"

"Why don't you have some fun?" urged the Grand Adviser.

"Good idea! But how do I have fun?" he asked.

No one in the palace could tell him, so he decided to go and look for fun across the land.

Great excitement spread throughout the kingdom when the Littlest Emperor's quest for fun became known. As he traveled, he learned that a great palace with a towering pagoda was being built for him. But he had a huge palace already, so that was no fun, and he continued on his journey.

When the Littlest Emperor stopped in a big city, a grand opera with beautiful costumes and wonderful music was performed. But it went on for too long and with a yawn he fell asleep. This wasn't what he was looking for at all! So he asked, "Isn't there another kind of fun? Where can I find it?" No one could tell him and so he continued on his way.

At the next stop in the largest town, poems only praising the Littlest Emperor were read. But he soon grew bored with hearing only about himself, and again he fell asleep.

He awoke to a banquet overflowing with delicious roast meats, bird's nest soup, exotic seafood including jellyfish noodles, juicy fruits, and fragrant Chinese tea. There was more food than anyone could possibly eat, so the Littlest Emperor wished for this feast to be shared with hungry people in other kingdoms.

Then he asked, "Isn't there another kind of fun? Where can I find it?"

No one in the town could tell him.

So he continued on his travels, searching everywhere, but he still couldn't find the fun he wanted!

Just as the Littlest Emperor was giving up hope of ever finding fun, his carriage became stuck in the thickest and deepest mud. Looking out of the window he saw lots of children in a rice field, and heard their loud shrieks and wild laughter. As guards hurriedly tried to free the carriage, the Littlest Emperor decided to sneak out to see what the children were doing.

Before anyone noticed him, the Littlest Emperor tossed off his clothes and jumped into the squishy mud with a big smile on his face, and headed towards the laughing and shrieking children. Suddenly.......

A mud ball hit him smack on the face! The Littlest Emperor hurled a mud ball back and soon hundreds of mud balls were whizzing all around. Rolling, sliding and laughing away, they were quickly covered in mud from head-to-toe! The Littlest Emperor didn't even hear the Grand Adviser calling him because he was having such a great time! This was really fun!

As the sun was setting, all of the children ran for home—and the Littlest Emperor followed! No one recognized him—he looked just like all the other mud-caked children.

WHEEEE! SPLISH!—SPLOSH!—SPLASH!

They all jumped into a giant bath tub. This was the first time the Littlest Emperor had shared a bath. He really enjoyed playing and relaxing with his new-found friends. Afterwards, the children were told to get ready for the Littlest Emperor's arrival and the Littlest Emperor put on village clothes with the rest of them.

"The Emperor is here! The Emperor is here!" the villagers called out as the carriage arrived. The carriage door opened, the Grand Adviser stepped out sobbing and the cheers stopped. He cried, "The Emperor is gone! The Emperor is lost!"

"No I'm not!" called out one of the children—it was the Littlest Emperor. "I'm here! And guess what? I've been playing in the mud! And I've found fun at last!"

"Fun? You call that fun?" asked the shocked Grand Adviser.

"Yes, mud fighting—you should try it!" shouted the Littlest Emperor as he hurled a mud ball in the air—the signal for the beginning of a new mud fight. The Grand Adviser was so happy to see the Littlest Emperor that he played and had fun too!

The village celebrated the Littlest Emperor's visit for three more days and nights. He discovered that there were lots of fun things to see and do—playing leap frog, spinning tops, skipping, flying kites.

There was a man walking on stilts so high that the Littlest Emperor could only see the bottom of his feet! Jugglers performed and the Littlest Emperor learned how to juggle too. Many times the balls fell on his head! BOOM...BOOM...BOOM...BOOM...BOOM......

BOOM! The children ran towards the sound of
roaring drums and joined a magical dragon dance.
The Littlest Emperor had the time of his life dancing
and jumping all around the village with his friends.

Eventually it was time for the Littlest Emperor to go home.
The Grand Adviser could hardly believe that it was in the smallest
village at the edge of the kingdom that the Littlest Emperor had
found the most fun! The Littlest Emperor and his new-found friends
visited each other for many years to come, and at the same time every
year, he returned to the village to celebrate the Festival of Friendship
and Fun!